# THE PENGUIN WHO WAS COLD

Philip Giordano

**T** tra.publishing

Brrr! Brrr! One morning Milo realized he was cold!

But Mom and Dad weren't cold.

And none of the other penguins were cold.

Every morning the penguins
went to the edge of the pack ice,
where the ice meets the sea.

There, they took turns diving
into the freezing cold ocean
in search of little fish to eat.

One day, Milo refused to jump. Even the thought
of plunging into the icy sea made him feel cold!
He stood there all alone staring into the frigid water.

"What's the matter?" a voice asked.
The penguin looked around, but
there didn't seem to be anyone there.
"Why aren't you in the sea with the others?"
asked the voice.

"Because I'm cold!" Milo said.

The water began to bubble.

"Hello!" said a whale. "I'm about to travel.
I think you would like the place where I'm going.
Would you like to come along?"

"Sure. As long as it isn't cold," Milo said.
He would rather jump on the whale's back
than dive into the glacial sea.

Flying fish saw them off,
flapping their wing-like fins
to wave goodbye to Milo.

They met a turtle who gave them directions.

But then, for days, they saw only water
and more water and more water
and a few small jellyfish.

"Are we lost?" Milo wondered.

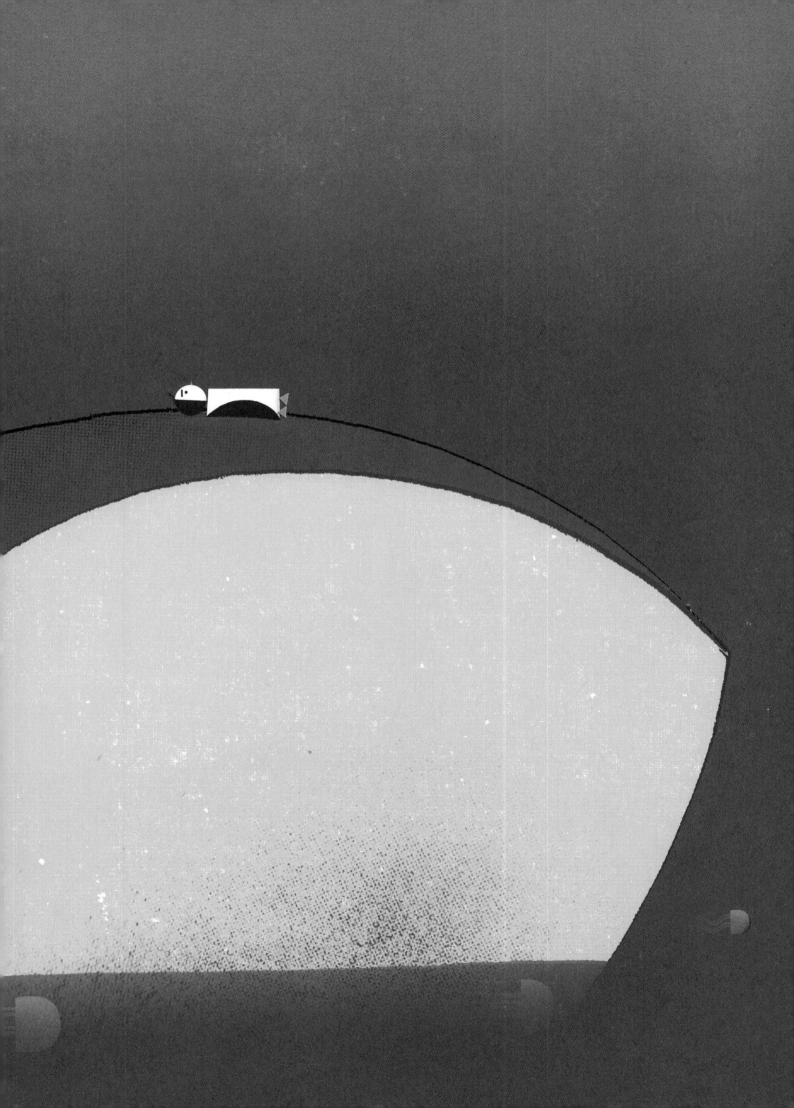

Finally, there it was! An island!

On the island,
birds of a thousand
colors and shapes
greeted the penguin
with a big welcome.

In the evening,
a large white parrot
invited Milo to see
the view from the tallest
tree on the island.

Beneath them, the jungle slept.
The silence was very familiar
to Milo. Pointing to the moon,
which looked like an igloo,
he began to talk about his home.

He spoke of the frozen pack ice,
of the snow that fell silently,
and of the fact that he had been
feeling cold for a long time.

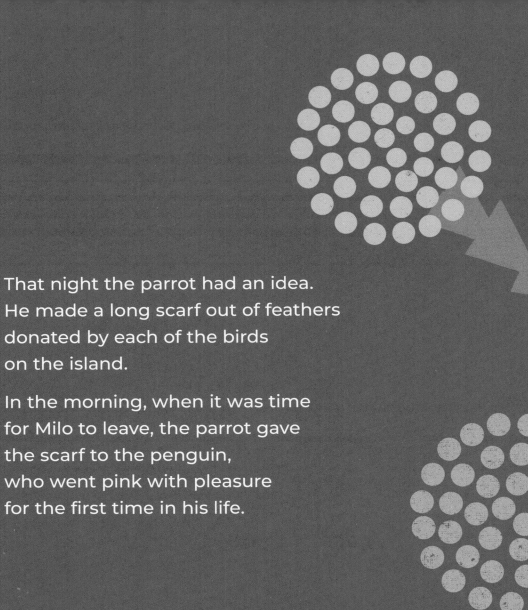

That night the parrot had an idea.
He made a long scarf out of feathers
donated by each of the birds
on the island.

In the morning, when it was time
for Milo to leave, the parrot gave
the scarf to the penguin,
who went pink with pleasure
for the first time in his life.

"Remember that you will always be welcome here,"
said the white parrot, waving to Milo from the beach.

The journey home seemed endless.
Finally the pack ice appeared.
Nothing seemed to have changed.

But thanks to the scarf, Milo realized
he was no longer cold.

Every morning the penguins
went to the edge of the pack ice,
where the ice meets the sea.

There, they took turns diving
into the freezing cold ocean
in search of little fish to eat.

One day, another penguin refused to jump.
The mere thought of plunging into the
glacial water made him feel cold.
Brrr! Brrr! So he stood there all alone
staring at the icy ocean.

"Hey, you! What's the matter?"
The penguin on the edge of the
pack ice turned and saw Milo.

And he understood he wasn't alone.

There were
other penguins
in the world
who didn't like
the cold.

And there was a whole world of wonders to discover.